AROUND THE WORLD IN 80 DAYS

Original story by Jules Verne
Retold by Rob Alcraft
Series Advisor Professor Kimberley Reynolds
Illustrated by Alex Paterson

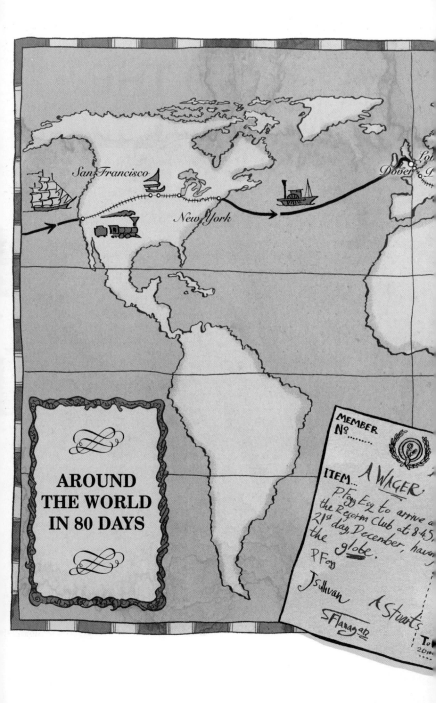

AROUND THE WORLD IN 80 DAYS

MEMBER Nº ....

ITEM... *A WAGER*

P. Fogg Esq to arrive a
the Reform Club at 8.45,
21st day, December, havin
the globe.
P. Fogg

J Sullivan   A Stuarts

S Flanagan

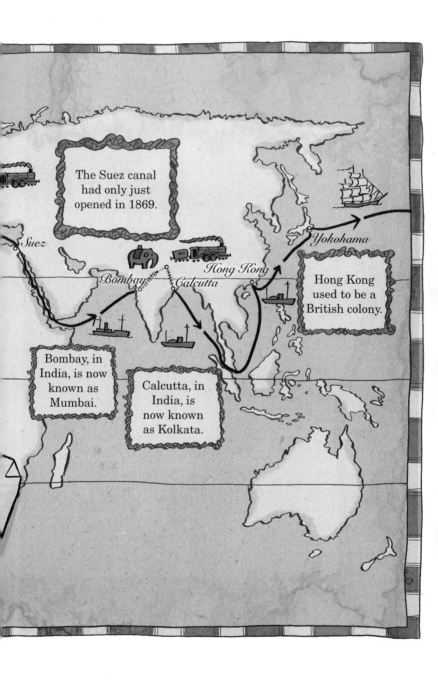

The Suez canal had only just opened in 1869.

Suez

Bombay

Calcutta

Hong Kong

Yokohama

Hong Kong used to be a British colony.

Bombay, in India, is now known as Mumbai.

Calcutta, in India, is now known as Kolkata.

Letter from the Author

Dear Traveller,

   You are holding exactly the right book. Start right away! This story has been waiting for you since it was first told, in French, in 1873. It's got robbery, adventure and a fair amount of what is best called trouble. There is even an elephant. What more could you ask for?

   I would certainly have welcomed an elephant trotting in when I was at school. It might have saved me from some of the extra spelling I had to do. My problem, my teacher told me, was that I just made it up as I went along.

   Happily, now that I'm a writer, I can make things up whenever I want, and my computer helps me with the spelling. So here I am, typing away in a maroon caravan in my garden, and the elefant – sorry elephant – is about to arrive. You had better get going ...

Rob Alcraft

In which a gentleman in a top hat vanishes

The crime was fiendishly simple, and over almost as soon as it began. Its blunt, swift violence alarmed all of London. It was as though the very heart of the nation had been twisted from its breast.

It was a tall man in a top hat, apparently a gentleman, with bushy whiskers and a curly moustache. He was seen in an upper corridor at the Bank of England at around four o'clock. Some minutes later, he entered the paying room.

On some pretence, the clerk had been persuaded to leave the room. The cashier was counting bank notes stacked across the table in front of him. He looked up, then returned to his work.

It was twenty-five feet across the room. The man moved quickly, reaching the table before the cashier even knew he was there. The cashier caught a brief glimpse of bushy whiskers and then saw that the man had raised his hand. He was holding something heavy and bringing it down fast.

When the clerk returned, the cashier was slumped forward over his table. The man in the top hat had gone, taking with him all the money in the room.

In which Phileas Fogg makes a wager

'Absolutely stunning!'

Flanagan slapped a card down onto the table, grinning round at his three companions.

Phileas Fogg, who was to play next, looked carefully at Flanagan's big pinkish face.

'It's a three,' he said. 'I wouldn't call it absolutely stunning.'

'Not the card, man!' said Flanagan. 'The robbery!'

The robbery was irregular and Fogg's day had been irregular enough already. Indeed, he had lost his servant after the man had apparently been overwhelmed by the folding of a sock. Now, in the comfortable surroundings of London's Reform Club, he had hoped to play a game of cards without a robbery galloping into it.

'Any news?' Flanagan persisted, turning now

to Stuarts and Sullivan, both directors at the bank.

'Our cashier was soundly clubbed,' said Sullivan. 'He barely knows his own name. Keeps mumbling about tall men with whiskers, moustaches and top hats. A bit like you, Fogg!'

Fogg smiled thinly.

'We'll catch the robber,' said Stuarts. 'We have detectives at all the European ports. He won't escape.'

'He's escaped already,' said Fogg, laying an ace over Flanagan's three. 'My game, I believe.'

'He has certainly not escaped,' scowled Flanagan. 'He shall be caught.'

Phileas Fogg raised a luxuriantly bushy eyebrow. 'He could be in Paris already, in Egypt in six days, Bombay inside two weeks. For goodness' sake, a man can go around the world in eighty days!'

'Pah!' said Flanagan.

'It's quite true,' said Sullivan. '*The Times* has said the same. Now the Indian railway is complete at Allahabad, it is possible.'

'Pah!' said Flanagan again.

'There's no "Pah!" about it,' said Fogg, coldly. 'It can be done in eighty days.'

'It can't!' said Flanagan, his voice rising.

'It can.'

'Well, Fogg, since you've nothing better to do, why don't you go around the world in eighty days? A thousand pounds says you can't!'

9

Fogg, shuffling the cards, was suddenly still. It was true, he didn't actually have anything better to do. He wondered, in fact, if anyone would particularly notice he had gone.

One thing was clear though, it would cost a lot more than a thousand pounds to make such a journey. He unfolded the possibilities in his mind carefully. The wager needed to be larger, so that when he won, he would at least be even.

'Twenty thousand,' said Fogg, 'and you're on.'

There was a stunned silence. This was a fortune so huge, on a bet so improbable, that it seemed Phileas Fogg must not be quite well.

'Phileas!' said Sullivan. 'Have you taken leave of your senses?'

Flanagan had turned rather more pink than usual. 'No! Fogg says he can; I say he can't! Twenty thousand pounds it is!'

'Very well,' said Fogg, getting to his feet.

'It is a quarter before nine on the second day of October.'

He put on his top hat.

'I will see you in this room in exactly eighty days. Goodnight, gentlemen.'

In which Phileas Fogg admires some folding

3

As Phileas Fogg left the Reform Club, it was not the eighty days ahead that worried him, but the seventy-two minutes before the train to Dover. It was all the time he had left, in which to find a new servant.

The events of the morning had been very trying. His servant had suggested, rather rudely, that if Fogg wanted his socks folded at a particular angle, he should do it himself.

'I,' the man had shrieked, running from the house, 'am not a sock!'

It had been a most peculiar remark.

Turning into Pall Mall, he began counting his footsteps. The regularity of it was pleasing. Usually it was 575 steps to his home. Tonight, he would need to visit his banker and he calculated it would take about 800 steps to get there, then 900 more to return home.

He would have to count to be sure.

In the event, it was 803 steps to his banker, who, though surprised, provided the £20,000 Fogg requested, packing it into a carpet bag.

Fogg set off towards his house in Saville Row. A slight boy, with a mess of hair and wearing rags, was selling newspapers at the corner.

'Robbery, sir? All the latest.'

'I've had quite enough of the robbery, thank you,' said Fogg.

'A big bash on the head, sir, it says here.'

The boy held up the paper, folding it over with a neat, easy skill. Fogg stopped.

Here was a boy who would be able to fold a sock, but might not need to run about shrieking while he did it.

He took the paper, admiring again the easy exactness of the fold.

'Your name?'

'Passepartout.'

'French?'

'No, sir. Orphan.'

'You could be useful?'

'Yes, sir. Often.'

'You see, I need a servant. That could be you?'

'Yes, sir!' said Passepartout.

'Mmm,' said Fogg. He remembered again the unpleasantness of the morning. It might be as well to deal with the sock issue straight away.

'I need my socks folded at a precise angle
– exactly once. Could you do that without
shouting?'

'Yes, sir,' said Passepartout, for he thought
that he probably could.

'Good,' said Fogg. 'The job is yours.'

He took out his notebook and, scribbling
something, tore out a page and gave it to
Passepartout.

'You will, I think, need some clothes. This
is my tailor's address and a note in case he finds
your appearance disturbing, which is quite
possible. He will also supply you with a watch.
You will need it.

'My address is 72 Saville Row. Don't be late!
We are going on a journey, Passepartout.'

Fogg strode off down the street, forgetting
to count his steps. When he remembered, it
was too late to start. The journey had hardly
begun and he was already adrift in
the unknown.

4

In which there is a firm intent to travel

The next six days were a whirl of trains, arrivals and departures.

Passing through Paris, Passepartout realized that life as a servant would not be what he had expected. Crossing into Italy, he decided it was even better. He saw Florence, if only briefly, and had a glimpse of Rome.

London

Paris

He carried Fogg's bag usefully and folded his socks correctly. Then, with Phileas Fogg tall and straight as a stick, his top hat firmly in place, they boarded a steamer at Naples and left Europe behind.

It was all rather easy, Passepartout decided. Only his new watch did not seem to be able to keep up. It was behaving oddly, losing time as they travelled east towards Suez.

Florence
Rome
Naples

In which some bushy whiskers display a definite criminal curl

On the morning of 9th October, the black hull of the *Mongolia* slid alongside the quay at Suez, its funnels belching smoke. Above the quay, in the doorway of the British Consul's office, Detective Fix stood watching through binoculars.

He studied a line of passengers on the upper deck.

'The robber is on that ship,' he said. 'I know it!'

'I don't see how you can know,' said the Consul.

There was a £5,000 reward on offer for the arrest of the Bank of England robber. The Consul wondered if Fix wasn't just a little too interested in it!

'The description is, rather general, isn't it?'

'It's very specific actually,' said Fix, still looking through his binoculars.

'What? Bushy whiskers and a top hat. And tall!'

'Exactly!'

'It could be just about anyone,' said the Consul.

'No,' said Fix. He turned. 'It doesn't fit me, does it?'

The detective was small and bald and wore no hat.

Fix raised the binoculars again. There were a number of gentlemen in top hats on the *Mongolia*. He studied them, looking now along the lower deck. He stopped. There was a figure in the shadows. The man stepped forward.

'There!' said Fix.

He squinted into the binoculars. The figure was tall and there was a definite criminal curl to his whiskers.

'He's coming this way!'

'Yes, he would be – with his passport,' observed the Consul, studying the back of Fix's little bald head. It occurred to him that once an idea had got lodged inside it, it might be difficult to get it out again.

'There's a boy with him,' said Fix. 'We'll keep them here, of course.'

'No, Detective Fix. As I've already explained, you have no warrant to arrest anyone.'

'Humph!' said Fix, stuffing the binoculars into his pocket. 'In that case, I don't want to be seen. Just don't let on you know who he is!'

'I don't know who he is.'

'Good! That's the spirit,' said Fix. 'I'm just going to get into this cupboard. Carry on!'

The Consul shook his head in disbelief as Detective Fix wedged himself into the cupboard that stood against the wall, leaving its door slightly ajar. A moment later, the tall figure from the lower deck appeared. He told the boy to wait, and entered the room. He smiled at the Consul, tipping his hat politely, holding out his passport. The Consul took it, flipping it open.

'You are Phileas Fogg?'

'Yes. Pleased to meet you.'

'Where are you travelling to?'

'London.'

There was a clank suddenly from inside the cupboard. Fogg glanced over at it, raising his eyebrows.

'I think someone may be trapped in your cupboard.'

'Unlikely,' said the Consul breezily. 'Anyway, you were saying?'

'Oh, yes,' said Fogg. 'I am travelling around the world – India, Hong Kong, Japan, America, then London.'

'It sounds most interesting,' said the Consul. He stamped the passport and held it out. 'Have a good journey.'

Fogg raised his hat, gave the cupboard a curious look and then was gone.

'Mmm,' said the Consul, watching Fix as he struggled out from his hiding place. 'He didn't seem particularly criminal.'

'It's him,' said Fix. 'I was watching. I know.'

Back at the doorway, Fix stared out after Phileas Fogg as he made his way towards the *Mongolia*. This was his man. All he needed now was a warrant for his arrest.

In which a shopkeeper's head is firmly trodden on

Back on board the *Mongolia*, Fogg offered the engineer a reward should they reach Bombay early. Then, calculating that he might fit in thirty-three games of cards, he went in search of someone to play them with.

Passepartout was left to lounge. The weather was calm and he passed a pleasant voyage making friends, in fact, with a small bald man who seemed very interested in their journey, and the contents of the carpet bag.

They arrived at Bombay two days early and went immediately to the railway station. There was an hour to spare and Fogg, seeing that Passepartout was restless, suggested that he go in search of socks.

Gratefully, Passepartout wandered off to explore the streets beyond the station. Colourful bales of cloth were piled in doorways.

Strange fruits were stacked on tables. He drank tea at a stall and then he happened upon a curious little shop selling socks. Remembering his errand, he stepped inside.

Passepartout peered around in fascination, making his way further into the shadowy interior. He did not notice the shopkeeper, who was laid out on the floor, taking a nap on a little mattress. Passepartout stepped forward and regrettably, but quite firmly, trod on the man's head.

The shopkeeper rose up yelling, and everything began to go badly wrong. For, with all the sudden noise, Passepartout rather panicked.

'Socks!' he cried, grabbing a nearby pair and waving them at the shopkeeper. 'I want socks!'

Unfortunately, this was not really the right thing to do. For the socks were so utterly hideous that waving them at anyone would have been rather rude. But Passepartout was waving them at someone whose head he had just been standing on. It was all too much. The shopkeeper uttered another loud yell and lunged forward.

Passepartout did the only thing he could think of. He ran.

At the train, Fogg was waiting.

'I was beginning to think I would have to leave you behind,' he said.

'I stood on a shopkeeper,' said Passepartout miserably, 'and I got these.'

Fogg's face creased in disgust.

'A gentleman's socks do not look like that!' he said. 'Put them away! I absolutely forbid you to bring them out unless I expressly request it.'

'Yes, Master,' said Passepartout. 'But I didn't actually get a chance to pay for them. He started chasing me and, well …'

'That is unfortunate,' said Fogg. 'Though I suggest there are few people alive who would have willingly paid for them either. Let us put the matter behind us.'

Yet it was not to be, for on a seat nearby, unseen, sat a small bald man. The warrant had not arrived, but now he'd had a useful idea. He slipped away from the platform. The matter of the socks would not be left behind so easily, he would make sure of it.

In which Phileas Fogg has a grand and brilliant idea

They had been winding through a hot, baked landscape of fields and hills for nearly three days when the train entered a dark, tangled forest and stopped.

Out of the window, Passepartout could see people getting off the train and heading into the forest, carrying their luggage. Jumping down from the train, Passepartout saw why. The forest ahead rose up in a wall. There was no more railway.

Passepartout was about to return and give Fogg this news when he caught sight of a large dark shape, half-hidden in the shadow of the trees. Something was in there, watching him.

* * *

'What exactly am I looking at, Passepartout?' Passepartout studied his master's face with some puzzlement. 'It's an elephant, Master.'

Phileas Fogg sighed heavily.

'Yes, Passepartout,' he said slowly. 'I can see the elephant. Indeed, there would have to be something rather wrong with me if I couldn't, don't you think? I was perhaps more interested to know for what reason I was looking at it. We do not have time, Passepartout, for elephants.'

'But, Master—' said Passepartout.

'Enough! We have a journey to make. While you have been idling, I have discovered that not only is there no more railway, but that our destination of Allahabad is a good day's journey from here.'

'Master, but that's—'

'Please, Passepartout, shhh!' said Fogg. 'I've just had a very fine idea. I think this creature might, in fact, carry us. 'It's a good thing that at least one of us has given some thought to the journey, isn't it?'

'Yes,' said Passepartout, sighing now himself. 'The owner's over there.'

'Excellent,' said Fogg, and he strode off towards the man, who sat resting under a tree. Passepartout trailed after him.

'My good man,' said Fogg, lifting his top hat. 'I would like to borrow your elephant.'

Half an hour later, Fogg found that it was, as it turned out, not possible to borrow an elephant. One had to buy it, and for an elephant-sized price.

Passepartout held open the carpet bag and watched in amazement as Fogg collected up £2,000.

'Don't worry, Passepartout!' said Fogg cheerfully. 'I have foreseen a number of large purchases, though I admit I did not imagine one of them might be an elephant. 'Though now I rather feel that every gentleman should have one. Isn't he a fine beast?'

They waited as a little bench was strapped onto the elephant's back. The beast obligingly knelt, so that Fogg and Passepartout could climb on. The driver was a boy, about Passepartout's age, who sat at the elephant's head.

'This is my good friend, Kiouni,' said the boy, smiling at his passengers. 'And I am Jai.'

They set off into the forest, unaware that by the time they left its dark tangle, nothing would be quite the same.

In which a horror is revealed among the tangled trees

They followed a series of paths, going deeper into the forest. Around them, the wall of trees hummed and buzzed with unseen insects.

They had been travelling several hours and the sun was setting when Kiouni became oddly restless. He raised his trunk and began to slow, then stopped.

'This is not good,' said Jai quietly. He listened into the growing darkness of the forest.

A long way off, faintly at first, came the sound of a strange, insistent drumming. As they listened, it grew louder, coming steadily closer.

'We must not be seen,' said Jai. 'I have heard of these people.'

He began to back the elephant off the path into the thick undergrowth.

The drumming was closer now, growing

more frantic as it wound towards them. There were wild cries and an eerie, meandering piping, reedy and high.

Soon the leaping flames of torches appeared in the darkness, snaking along the path. They could see the men's faces, bearded and fierce, the drummers swaying rhythmically, the noise filling the forest around them.

Then they saw the woman. She was dressed as a bride, her robe shimmering with gold and yet there was a rope around her neck. She was being drawn like an animal through the darkening forest.

She stumbled, but was dragged onwards, the horrible procession passing along the path, the dancing flames of the torches dipping and twisting onwards, the drumming and shouts growing fainter, receding into the forest.

'What villainy is this?' hissed Fogg. 'Who is she, to be led by the neck?'

'She is the Princess Aouda,' said Jai.
'Everyone here has heard of her. She has
refused to marry the bandit king. He killed her
father, and she will never marry him.'

'But what will happen to her?' said
Passepartout.

The boy did not answer immediately.

'What will happen?' said Passepartout
again. 'Tell me.'

'I did not believe it,' said Jai, 'but I see it is true. They will burn her when the sun rises. This is what they have promised.'

'Burn her?' said Passepartout. 'But—'

'We go on, Mr Fogg?' said Jai. 'In two hours, we can reach Allahabad.'

They had almost turned onto the path, the moon rising behind them, bathing them in silvery light.

'No,' said Fogg. 'That way.'

He pointed along the path, back towards the princess.

In which a princess must be rescued

They followed the path through the forest, listening to the soft tread of the elephant and, always ahead of them, the beat of the drums.

The night had nearly passed when they reached the edge of a wide clearing and the drumming stopped. At the other side of the clearing, the bandits began to drag wood and branches from the forest. Then, as the first sharp rays of the sun cut through the clearing, they brought the princess forward, forcing her up onto the pyre of wood, tethering her with ropes. One of the men passed a flaming brand around the base of the pyre. Smoke began to curl upwards.

The three travellers crouched by Kiouni at the edge of the clearing, watching in horror. Suddenly Fogg sprang upright.

'I'm not having it!' he said. 'This simply won't do!'

With that, Phileas Fogg strode out into the open.

He was halfway across the clearing before the bandits saw him.

One of them jeered, baring his teeth. Fogg walked on, towards the men and the fire.

'They will kill him!' said Jai.

The smoke had thickened now, swirling up around the princess.

'The elephant!' said Passepartout. 'Kiouni!'

Jai was on his feet and, with one step, was climbing up onto Kiouni's neck. Then he was reaching down and pulling Passepartout after him, so that in a moment they were on Kiouni's back, crashing from the edge of the forest and charging forward.

They gathered pace in lumbering strides, passing Fogg, charging on towards the fire.

The appearance of the elephant threw the

men into confusion. There were urgent shouts. Then Kiouni was upon them, the great beast bearing down. The bandits scattered.

Passepartout felt the fire – a wall of flame, smoke thick and blinding. The princess was dragging against the ropes, wrenching herself free. Then she was drawn upwards, Kiouni's trunk curling tightly around her, lifting her away and onto his back.

They crashed on through the fire and out, burning branches scattering around them, as they thundered back across the clearing towards Fogg. The bandits had gathered themselves. An arrow sang past Passepartout's head.

Reaching Fogg, Kiouni slowed just long
enough to curl his trunk around him, and
still rushing forward, lifted Fogg up over his
head to safety. Arrows sang and zipped around
them, but a moment more and they were into
the trees, plunging on, the shouts of the men
dying into the distance behind them.

'I say!' exclaimed Fogg, reaching across
the lurching elephant to shake the startled
princess's hand. 'I say! Capital! Welcome
aboard! Onward, Kiouni! Onward to
Allahabad. We've a train to catch!'

In which Phileas Fogg has finished with his elephant

They rode into Allahabad, right to the station, by elephant.

A train was waiting. People were climbing on board, passing bundles up through the windows.

'I have finished with my elephant,' Fogg declared grandly, smiling at Jai. 'He is yours.'

The boy was still too overjoyed to speak when they boarded the train a few minutes later.

As they set off, he climbed up onto Kiouni's neck and trotted along by the track, waving as the train gathered speed and began to pull away.

Looking back through the open window, Princess Aouda smiled.

'You are a strange pair of travellers,' she said. 'You rescue me from fire in the morning and, in the afternoon, you give away elephants! Mr Fogg, do you always do such kind and impressive things?'

'No,' said Fogg, thoughtfully. 'But perhaps I should.'

Passepartout liked Princess Aouda immediately. She called him her daring young man. Fogg seemed delighted to have her company too, not least because she proved rather good at cards. When he discovered she had no close family left in India, but an uncle in London, he immediately invited her to accompany them.

They reached Calcutta on the morning of 25th October. They had lost the two days they had in hand from the sea voyage to Bombay, but had gained instead a princess.

Passepartout followed Fogg and Aouda down from the train, still flushed with the success of the rescue, only to find four policemen awaiting them, their silver buttons shining.

'Passepartout? Phileas Fogg?' said one, stepping forward. 'You are under arrest.'

In which Phileas Fogg expressly requests a pair of socks

Phileas Fogg, gentleman and member of the Reform Club, and Passepartout, his servant, stood in the dock of Calcutta's criminal court. Aouda sat anxiously behind.

The strange matter of a pair of socks from Bombay had not, it seemed, been forgotten. Rather surprisingly, it had followed them all the way across India, together with a bruised and angry shopkeeper.

'This is a serious matter,' said the judge. 'You must expect a custodial sentence.'

Above, in the gallery, a small bald man watched unseen, a smile creeping across his little round face.

'Do you have anything to say?' asked the judge.

'Yes, Your Honour,' said Fogg, standing forward. He looked slowly round the courtroom.

'The horror!' he said finally. 'The horror of it!'

There was a murmur around the court.

Fogg paused, letting the words hang, whispering to Passepartout, who reached into the carpet bag.

'Exhibit one!' said Fogg, holding up the socks, stored, as instructed, until requested. He shook out their folds, exposing the full horror of their design.

There was a gasp, for the socks were indeed a most unusual and disturbing sight.

'To meet these!' hissed Fogg. 'Without warning! These!' said Fogg again, shaking the socks in his fist, his voice. 'These! In the dark of a shop, such stripe and dreadfulness!

'I tell you,' said Fogg, his voice now low and thick, 'that these socks triggered a panic in my servant's young mind. A fever of fear!'

Fogg swung his gaze now to the shopkeeper, who found suddenly that everyone else was looking at him too. He hung his head. He wished that he had never listened to the small bald detective or taken the £50 to pursue the case and was indeed back in his shop, lying quietly on the floor.

'You, sir, are a disgrace!' said Fogg.

There was an angry murmur of agreement in the court. Fogg addressed the judge.

'My servant is guilty only of a dreadful panic. I urge the court to set him free!'

The judge lent forward to confer with the court's lawyers.

'Your actions were foolish,' said the judge eventually, 'but the court accepts that the socks are shocking. I propose a fine. Mind you, it is substantial – £2000. Can you pay?'

Passepartout's mouth fell open. He had thought a few days before that this was a lot of money for an elephant. Now the elephant seemed a bargain.

'Yes, we can pay,' said Fogg easily. He took up the carpet bag and counted out a pile of notes.

Up in the gallery, the smile had entirely left Detective Fix's face.

'You are free to go,' said the judge. 'Next!'

'Oh, well done!' said Aouda, jumping up in delight. 'Mr Fogg, you are quite the lawyer!'

'Thank you,' said Fogg, smiling modestly.

Less than an hour later, they were aboard the deck of the *Rangoon*, making ready to sail for Hong Kong. They should arrive by 6th November. Fogg added the new date into his notebook. Thus occupied, he did not notice a small bald man on the gangplank below, hurrying on board.

In which Passepartout does the best thing possible

It was Passepartout who recognized the little bald man. They were due in Hong Kong later in the day and, while Fogg and Aouda played cards, Passepartout had decided to have a last look around the ship.

He saw Fix, leaning over the rail, trying to steady himself as the ship dipped and slid in the waves. He looked very seasick.

Fix had been on their ship from Suez. He had said he was stopping at Bombay. Now here he was again.

It was too curious.

'Ah! Mr Fix, what a surprise!'

'Oh!' said Fix, starting. 'You're here again.'

'Mmm!' said Passepartout. 'It's more that *you're* here again, isn't it? I know what you're up to!'

'You do?' said Fix, alarmed.

'Yes!' said Passepartout. 'You're following my master. You're from that Reform Club of his, aren't you?'

'Oh!' said Fix, pleased with this excellent explanation. 'You're too clever for me! You're right, the Reform want me to make sure your Phileas Fogg makes his journey and is safe doing it!'

'You're not here to stop him then?' said Passepartout, confused. 'I saw you skulking about and I thought—'

'I'm not skulking,' said Fix. 'I am unwell. Anyway, you don't imagine you escaped prison in Calcutta because of your master's fine words, do you?'

'That was you?' Passepartout was stunned.

'It was me. I spoke to the right people.'

Fix looked at Passepartout carefully, his brain whirring. The boy could be useful. He had to arrest Fogg on British soil and

Hong Kong was his last chance. He could collect the warrant and then Passepartout would lead him straight to his man.

'I have another way to help you, you know,' he said. 'Meet me – I have an errand when we land, but afterwards. There's a restaurant above the harbour. But don't tell your master,' said Fix. 'I don't imagine a man such as Fogg would like anyone looking after him.'

Passepartout thought for a moment. This was probably true. He nodded.

'Good,' said Fix. 'You're doing the best thing possible.'

But, of course, it was not the best thing possible. It was, in fact, the very worst.

In which there is a curious blue dragon

They arrived at Hong Kong that afternoon. A ring of forested hills rose up around the wide, busy harbour.

Fogg found the steamer agent and booked cabins on board the *Carnatic*, which was leaving for Japan the next morning.

'Splendid!' said Fogg. 'You wanted to see Hong Kong, Aouda, now we have time.'

They arranged to meet Passepartout later and walked off down the dock together.

Passepartout had spotted Fix's restaurant above the harbour. He had just set off towards it, when the steamer agent came hurrying up.

His information had been mistaken; the *Carnatic* would actually leave that night. Would the young gentleman deliver the message? Passepartout said that he would.

At the restaurant Fix was waiting. Two

bowls of green tea sat steaming on the table in front of him.

'I've ordered tea,' said Fix, looking at Passepartout carefully. 'Have some.'

The arrest warrant had still not arrived. Somehow Fix needed to keep Fogg in Hong Kong till it did. The boy was now in the way. He needed dealing with.

'You said you could help my master,' said Passepartout, sitting down.

He reached for one of the bowls, but Fix shook his head, pushing the other one forward. A blue Chinese dragon curled around the white porcelain.

'This one is yours,' said Fix.

'Oh,' said Passepartout, taking the bowl. 'So, how can you help?'

'Have some tea,' said Fix again. 'I'll tell you.'

Fix lifted his own bowl and drank.

Passepartout sipped at the tea. It tasted sharp and odd. He supposed that this was

how people liked their tea in Hong Kong.
He drank.

He needed to find Fogg and tell him about
the *Carnatic*. He would not stay long.

In which Passepartout remembers something important

It was dark when Passepartout woke, if it could be called waking. For he had not the least idea how he came to be lying in the street, his face pressed into a mush of rotting cabbage.

He groaned and crawled forward. Then, through the whirl in his head, he had a sudden, urgent memory.

He pulled himself dizzily to his feet. It was very important that he get on a ship.

Twenty minutes later, he was indeed on a ship. It was even the right ship. It was just that he was quite alone.

* * *

It was seven days across the South China Sea to Yokohama in Japan.

Passepartout lay in his bunk, feeling dreadful. He remembered drinking tea, but that was all. He knew only that he had failed his master and it would cost Fogg everything.

At Yokohama, Passepartout waited, but no passenger steamers came. The boat for America left the next day. If Fogg and Aouda did not arrive, everything was lost.

Passepartout slept in a luggage shelter next to the ticket agent's office on the harbour. A strange dream came. A tall man with curious blue eyes and bushy whiskers was wrestling a troll on the edge of a steep, high cliff. Passepartout wanted to help and stepped forward, but as he did so, he saw the tall man slip and begin to fall.

In which Passepartout is twice surprised

Passepartout felt himself gently shaken and opened his eyes cautiously. Since waking with his face in the gutter, he was never entirely sure what he might find.

But he need not have worried for it was Aouda smiling down at him and with her, the tall, bearded figure of Phileas Fogg.

Passepartout leapt up and embraced Aouda and then, not feeling that anyone had ever embraced Fogg, settled for grabbing his hand and shaking it vigorously.

61

Aouda told him excitedly of how Fogg had found a ship to carry them and of the gigantic storm that had engulfed them.

Passepartout apologized again and again for causing them to miss the *Carnatic*.

'It is all behind us and is forgotten,' said Fogg, his eyes twinkling. 'Onwards!'

Happily reunited, they boarded the *General Grant*, which was leaving to cross the Pacific Ocean to America.

Passepartout busied himself with a supply of Fogg's socks which, insufficiently folded, had gone unworn. He talked more with Aouda and it was then that she told him about the small bald man who had travelled with them from Hong Kong.

So it was, that while walking on deck later, Passepartout found himself meeting once again with Mr Fix.

In which Fix makes things up

'Oh! We meet again!' said Fix, startled. 'I thought you were lost to us! What happened?'

If the boy remembered anything, this was going to be difficult. Fix looked at the ship's rail. He might well have to tip the boy over it.

'I don't know what happened,' said Passepartout. 'I thought you might know!'

'You don't remember?' Fix felt a flood of relief. Now he could make things up, which would be a little easier than wrestling Passepartout into the Pacific.

'You were very odd,' said Fix.

'Was I?' said Passepartout.

'Oh yes! You drank your tea and then I'm afraid you were rather rude about it, and then you walked off!'

'Really?' said Passepartout. 'You just let me

wander off?'

'I'm not a policeman, am I?' said Fix smiling.
'I couldn't very well stop you. Besides, I thought
you'd gone back to your master. But you hadn't,
had you? You'd left us in the lurch and we all
missed the *Carnatic* because of you!'

Fix smiled again. He was enjoying himself.

'Anyway, it was all for the best. I got to know
your master and he's now invited me to travel
with you. I can be around to help all the time!'

GENERAL GRANT

'Oh,' said Passepartout. Somehow this didn't feel like a good thing.

Passepartout was, of course, quite right. For helping was not exactly what Fix had in mind. His warrant had finally arrived; it had been waiting at Yokohama. Now he just needed to stay close to Fogg and then, once they were back on British soil, he could arrest him.

The despicable criminal, Fogg, would not escape him now.

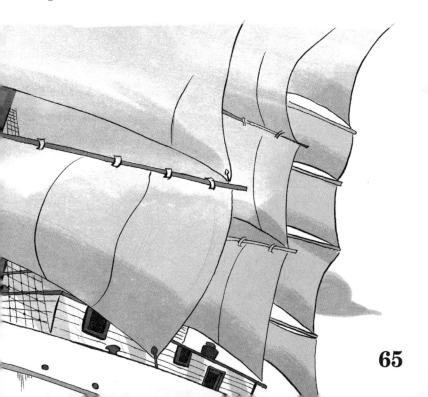

In which robbers pursue a train

They arrived in San Francisco on 2nd December and boarded a train headed east. They had fourteen days to reach New York and the last ship to England.

The train crossed through mountains and then, after several days, descended onto a wide, snow-covered prairie.

Their carriage was arranged like a long room, with tables and comfortable chairs. They sat and talked and Fogg insisted on a game of cards.

'I hope you're watching, Passepartout,' said Aouda as she and Fogg played one afternoon. 'I am teaching our dear Mr Fogg how to lose!'

'Mmm,' said Fogg. 'We'll see.'

They began another game.

Passepartout leaned his head on the window, looking out over the prairie. The

snow blew and drifted on in an endless, empty
sea of white. Except it wasn't empty.

There were men on horses, appearing from
a deep gulley a little way from the tracks,
riding hard, pulling level quickly with their
carriage at the rear of the train. Passepartout
craned his neck to see back along the carriage.
Two of the riders were leaning out, grabbing
at the handrails and swinging themselves from

their horses. They were boarding the train.

'Master!' said Passepartout, starting from his chair.

One of the riders was level with them now, a scarf over his face, his hat pulled forward against the snow. He raised something in his hand. There was a loud crack of gunfire. A window shattered and the carriage filled with a swirling confusion of snow and cards. At the rear of the carriage, a door burst open.

'Robbers!' shouted Fogg. 'To the next carriage! Move!'

At the door, one of the robbers aimed his gun. Bullets flew about them. Fogg's hat spun off suddenly into the air and Fix yelped, gripping his shoulder and turning suddenly pale.

'I say!' said Fogg.

Wedging his hat back on his head, he lifted one of the tables and, using it as a shield, they backed away down the carriage, bullets zinging around them. Reaching the door, they bundled through it, barring it behind them.

'That bolt!' shouted Fogg over the rush of the train, pointing down between the carriages. 'Passepartout, can you loosen it? Unhitch the carriage!'

Fogg and Aouda, holding the wounded Fix upright, hoisted him across the gap and on into safety.

Passepartout stretched down into the blur of snow, tugging at the heavy bolt, wrenching it back and forth. His fingers, clumsy in the cold, fumbled on the metal. Even over the wind and clatter of wheels, he could hear the robbers beating at the door.

He pulled harder and the bolt moved, sliding up, coming free.

Passepartout pulled himself upright. Across the gap, Fogg and Aouda had reappeared. But the carriage was slowing now, the gap widening.

'Jump,' shouted Fogg. 'Passepartout, now!'

He held out his hand across the growing gap, the tracks rushing away between them. It was four feet, five feet, more.

'Now!'

'Come on!' shouted Aouda.

But the moment was gone. It was too far. The train sped on, disappearing into the snow-covered distance.

In which Phileas Fogg does not hesitate

Passepartout knew he was probably lucky, but did not feel it. The robbers had taken his watch and left him, riding off across the snow.

The watch, he supposed, had not been much good anyway. It had been running oddly slow, as if it could not keep up as they travelled round the world.

He sat shivering, wrapping himself in curtains against the cold as the wind howled through the carriage.

* * *

Aouda told Passepartout later that Fogg had not hesitated in his resolve to go back for him, whether it would cost the wager or not.

Then Fix, who had not been seriously injured by the robbers, had found the strange prairie sled, rigged with mast and sails. They had come sliding out across the snow to the rescue.

Fogg had come back, but in doing so, they reached Omaha almost twenty hours behind. They took the first available train and were in Chicago by the evening of the 10th. They travelled through Indiana, Ohio and Pennsylvania.

Curiously, they began to pass through stations without stopping. Passepartout

could see bewildered people gesturing angrily after them.

'The driver knows where we have to be and by when,' said Fogg. 'And he knows his reward.'

So it was, that they covered the 900 miles from Chicago, to arrive over the Hudson River, and into New York. They stopped at the very quay where they found that the *China*, the last passenger ship that could get them to England, had left just three quarters of an hour before.

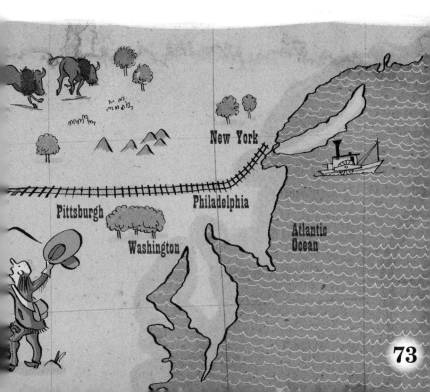

In which Phileas Fogg declares himself a desperate man

Mere ships would not stop Phileas Fogg now. The *China* had sailed, so he secured a fast cargo ship, the *Henrietta*.

It did not even matter that the *Henrietta*, or more particularly, the enormous Captain Speedy, would not sail for Liverpool, but made instead for France. Fogg simply paid the crew to lock the captain in his cabin and took over the ship.

It did not even seem to matter when, six days out into the rolling Atlantic, they began to run out of coal.

'Have the captain brought up, will you, Passepartout?'

'Master? Are you sure? He's still, well ... angry,' said Passepartout, for indeed the captain was often to be heard roaring and swearing. It seemed that he had never quite got used to the idea of being locked up on his own ship.

'Quite sure,' said Fogg.

It took four of the larger sailors to wrestle Captain Speedy into the wheelhouse, and, for safety's sake, tie him to a chair.

'We are running out of coal,' said Fogg. 'Unfortunately, it will be necessary for me to burn parts of your ship instead.'

Fogg smiled down at Speedy understandingly.

'I thought I'd better let you know before I started.'

This was a new outrage, so gigantic, that Captain Speedy had trouble taking it in. His face began to swell oddly.

'The wooden bits, anyway,' said Fogg. 'The hull is iron, and besides, we'll need something to float on, won't we?'

Captain Speedy's face turned purple. Finally he let out a long, incoherent howl.

Fogg stepped forward, leaning down, his eyes glinting.

'I can see that you are upset,' he said. 'But I am a desperate man. I must get to Liverpool and from there, to London in three days from now. If I do not then I am ruined. I would like to buy your ship and this would appear an ideal time for you to sell it because it will be burned.'

'You monster!' roared Speedy. 'You pirate! $40,000 this lady cost me! You hoof-foot! You—'

'Sixty,' said Fogg, cutting him off. 'I'll not give less.'

Fogg opened the carpet bag, and tipped out the last of the £20,000.

'Pounds, I'm afraid, but at current exchange, $60,323.'

The giant Speedy stared down at the money, a curious calm descending over him. At this price, he could have his ship rebuilt twice over.

'The hull,' said Speedy, 'that will be mine?'

'Of course,' said Fogg.

'And the engine?'

'Of course.'

'Captain!' said Speedy. 'She is yours!'

'Thank you, sir,' said Fogg, lifting his hat. 'Engineer, full steam ahead!'

There and then, a frenzy of destruction began, Speedy joining in with enthusiasm, as Passepartout, Aouda and the crew sawed and ripped and broke.

Only Fix did not join in. He lay seasick and groaning on his bunk, until that was sawn up, when he lay groaning on the floor, until finally his cabin was broken up too and he retreated down into the hull. There he lay groaning against one of the iron bulkheads, the thud of the engines, racing on at Fogg's command, drumming through his skull.

They stepped ashore at Liverpool with the mail train for London waiting. They had only to get on board.

In which Phileas Fogg finds himself attached

Passepartout set off at a run, Aouda behind him.

The mail train was fifty yards off, steam and smoke hissing around the engine. There were just six hours left to reach London. This was the last train possible.

'Come on!' Passepartout yelled. 'Come on!'

Fogg, striding after him, felt a hand on his arm and heard the clink of metal.

'Phileas Fogg?'

Fogg turned and saw that it was Fix. He felt Fix's hand sliding down towards his wrist.

'Perhaps you might let go of my arm,' said Fogg, still striding forward. Fix's grip tightened.

Fogg tried to wrench his arm away, but there was the sudden cold grip of metal around his wrist.

'Phileas Fogg, you are under arrest.'

Passepartout had reached the train. He was holding open one of the doors, Aouda next to him. Along the platform, the guard raised a flag. There were two shrill blasts of a whistle.

'Master! Come on!' Passepartout was waving, beckoning Fogg on. 'The train!'

Fogg shook at his arm, but felt the tug of the handcuffs as Fix stepped back.

'Fix, you are absurd!' said Fogg. 'Arrested

for what?'

'Detective Fix, to you, Fogg, and you know very well what for! It's over Fogg. You're done!'

The train had begun to move.

'Master!' shrieked Passepartout. 'The train! Come on!'

Passepartout was running now, still holding the door, trying to keep up as the train gathered speed.

Fogg looked down at Fix. He had travelled upon elephants and transport of all kinds. He had rescued princesses, he had burned ships, but he could not board a moving train while attached to a policeman, not even a small one that he had brought with him himself. It was beyond him.

The train gave a final whistle, the last carriage near the end of the platform, the tracks clacking.

'Master!' screamed Passepartout.

Phileas Fogg watched the train gathering speed, smelt the coal smoke, acrid and sour. A matter of fifty yards, when he had travelled so far. It was a distance he could not cross. The train was gone.

In which socks remain unfolded

Fix discovered six hours later that the Bank of England robber had been arrested at Dover the day before.

It made no difference. It was past a quarter to nine and the eighty days had passed. The wager was lost.

It was Fix himself who unlocked Fogg's cell. Fogg walked by him as though he wasn't there.

Fogg left arrangements for the journey to London with Passepartout. On the train, he sat looking out into the darkness.

He did not speak until they were approaching London when he looked gently at Aouda.

'I had hoped,' he said slowly. 'I had hoped that ... I am sorry, it is nothing. I mean only that I have been a fool.'

'Not all the time,' said Aouda. She put her hand over his.

London was very busy, but Fogg took no notice. At his home in Saville Row, he retired to bed immediately.

'I will pack my things tomorrow,' he said as he went up the stairs. 'We will need to leave the house. It is no longer mine.'

For most of the next day, Passepartout sat with Aouda in the living room, listening to Fogg upstairs, thumping about as he packed.

By the evening, Fogg had worked his way down to the living room. He shuffled through papers, throwing things onto the fire.

Eventually, Passepartout, beginning to feel in the way, got up.

'Master, I think I may go and fold your socks.'

Fogg looked at him and shook his head.

'No,' he said quietly. 'There will be no more

folding of socks, Passepartout. I shall simply wear them as they are.'

Passepartout sat down, feeling a little stunned.

Aouda raised her eyebrows and looked at Fogg with surprise. Then a shy smile appeared on her face, as though, at that moment, she had decided something of which she had been uncertain, but of which she was now sure.

'Phileas,' she said, getting up and taking a pile of papers out of his hands, 'I need to speak with you. Passepartout, would you give us a little time to talk?'

Passepartout left the room and waited, only to find that the door burst open again less than a minute later, Fogg and Aouda hand in hand, and then Passepartout found that Aouda had lifted him up and was swinging him round.

'We are to be married,' she laughed. 'Oh Passepartout, it's wonderful!'

'I have nothing at all,' said Fogg, laughing too. 'But I have everything!'

He took Aouda in his arms and, since she was still holding Passepartout, swung them both about the room.

'Go and find us a priest, Passepartout! I doubt they'll marry us on a Sunday, but we can always try!'

Still a little giddy from all the swinging about, Passepartout raced down into the street.

In which Passepartout breaks the tea things and Sunday is not Sunday

Fogg was sitting with Aouda. They were drinking tea and smiling at each other when the door burst open.

The next instant, Passepartout raced wildly into the room, tripping on the carpet as he came and sprawling into Fogg's little table of tea things. The cups and saucers smashed off into the air while Passepartout slid into a heap at Fogg's feet.

There was a moment of silence and a final tinkle of breaking china.

'Passepartout!' said Fogg. 'This is too much! You have broken my tea things.'

Passepartout shook his head, his eyes wide.

'You can't get married. You can't!'

'We can get married, thank you, Passepartout, and we will.'

He reached across and squeezed Aouda's hand.

'There will always be a place for you in our home; you don't need to be jealous.'

But Passepartout was now off the floor and climbing onto Fogg. For some peculiar reason, he was grabbing the front of Fogg's coat and trying to drag him from his chair.

'You can't!' gasped Passepartout again. 'It's not Sunday. It's Saturday!'

He looked desperately at Aouda. 'Help me!'

'Passepartout!' said Fogg. 'Do let go of my coat! It is not Saturday. I, of all people, know what day it is.'

'The priest said he can't do a wedding tomorrow because it's a Sunday,' wailed Passepartout. 'Today is Saturday! It's Saturday! It just is! Come on!'

Passepartout caught sight of the clock behind Fogg's head and let out another wail. They had until a quarter to nine. There were nine minutes left. Nine minutes left to save everything.

Aouda was looking at the clock too and had got to her feet.

'If it is Saturday,' she said, 'it means you can still reach the Reform Club. Foggy, the wager is yours!'

'Yes!' shrieked Passepartout. 'Yes!'

'But it simply can't be Saturday,' said Fogg, trying to hold his tea cup steady as Passepartout's tugging became still more frantic. 'If it was Saturday, it would mean that by travelling around the world we had gained time. It would ... '

Fogg stopped.

'It would mean,' said Fogg slowly, 'that we had gained a day.'

With a sudden jolt, he was on his feet, sending Passepartout tumbling back onto the floor and sloshing tea down into his face.

'Of course! It's obvious,' said Fogg. 'Why didn't I see?'

'Foggy,' said Aouda urgently. 'We need to go.'

'Of course!' said Fogg, not listening. 'Our journey took us east in the direction of the Earth's rotation! We chased the sunrise. We did gain time! For every day we travelled, we've gained eighteen minutes of time!'

Passepartout had picked himself up once more and was now trying to shove Fogg across the room to the door.

'Foggy!' said Aouda, louder. 'We need to go!'

Her eyes were on the clock. There were just eight minutes more.

'Every day travelling we've gained eighteen minutes. For eighty days. That's twenty-four hours! We did gain a day. We—'

'Fogg! Move!' yelled Aouda. She grabbed a great handful of Fogg's bushy whiskers, ignored his sudden shouts and began to haul him across the room. Passepartout gave a heave and together they bundled Fogg, still holding his tea cup, through the door, down the stairs and out onto the street.

There were just seven minutes left.

In which there is a man, a boy and a princess

A mile away at the Reform Club, Flanagan got to his feet.

'Six minutes!' he said, standing before the clock.

He had hardly kept still since first joining Sullivan and Stuarts in the main salon, two hours before.

'Oh, for goodness sake, man! Sit down,' said Stuarts.

'Pah!' said Flanagan, pacing off across the room.

He stopped at the window and lifted a corner of the heavy curtain so that he could look down onto street below.

A crowd had gathered and grown steadily larger, drawn by news of the immense fortune that was about to change hands. A sizeable mob now filled Pall Mall.

Flanagan let the curtain fall and turned back into the room.

'Three minutes!' he said. 'He will not be here. His project was absurdly foolish. Even he must have known it.'

He frowned.

'That ship – the *China*? You said it was the last possible way from New York and Fogg wasn't on it.'

'I said he wasn't on the passenger list,' said Sullivan. 'With Fogg that might well not be the same thing.'

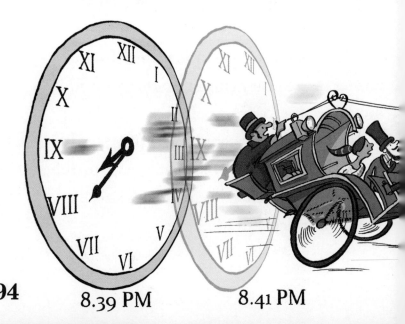

8.39 PM   8.41 PM

'Pah!' said Flanagan again, turning away from the clock.

He sat down. He got up, pacing once more down the room.

'Two minutes,' said Flanagan, watching the hands move. 'Less! Gentlemen, it's over, time has run through. Fogg is not here. I win!'

No one answered. They looked now only at the clock. There was one minute more.

Thirty seconds more.

And then, outside, a wave of noise began to rise from the crowd.

Fifteen seconds more.

8.43 PM

The hands ticked on. Five seconds.

Then, at one second before fifteen minutes to nine, the door opened and with a calm regular step, Phileas Fogg of 72 Saville Row, entered the room. He was holding a fine bone china tea cup, his top hat was on his head, and by his side were a boy and a princess.

'Gentlemen,' said Phileas Fogg. 'I am here. *We* are here!'